PICTURE BOOK THEATER

by Beatrice Schenk de Regniers

The Mysterious Stranger

The Magic Spell

illustrated by
William Lahey Cummings

CLARION BOOKS
TICKNOR & FIELDS : A HOUGHTON MIFFLIN COMPANY
NEW YORK

Clarion Books
Ticknor & Fields, a Houghton Mifflin Company
Text copyright © 1982 by Beatrice Schenk de Regniers
Illustrations copyright © 1982 by William Lahey Cummings

Text first registered in the copyright office PAu 124-909 1979
Printed in the United States of America

Designed by Mary Jane Dunton

Library of Congress Cataloging in Publication Data

de Regniers, Beatrice Schenk. Picture book theater:
    the mysterious stranger, the magic spell.
Summary: In these two plays about magic, a wicked witch imprisons
a princess and a wizard transforms a boy into a cat.
1. Children's plays, American. [1.Plays. 2.Magic—Drama]
I.Cummings, William Lahey, ill. II.Title.
PS3554.E66M9   812'.54   81-38495
ISBN 0-89919-061-8   AACR2

For

Carey

Christopher

Nimrod

Michal

Sigal

Ronnen

Lior

Tara

Joshua

Andrew

Juliet

Sarah

Daniel S.

Daniel X.

Other Clarion Books by Beatrice Schenk de Regniers

Everyone Is Good for Something
Illustrated by Margot Tomes

Little Sister and the Month Brothers
Illustrated by Margot Tomes

A Bunch of Poems and Verses
Graphics by Mary Jane Dunton

It Does Not Say Meow
and Other Animal Riddle Rhymes
Illustrated by Paul Galdone

Catch a Little Fox
Variations on a Folk Rhyme
Illustrated by Brinton Turkle

There are two plays in this book.

You can put on a puppet show.
Or you and your friends can be the actors.
Or you can enjoy reading the plays and
looking at the pictures—just as if you were
seeing the plays on TV or in a theater.

I am the narrator.
Sometimes I tell you what is happening.

Sometimes I answer questions.

Sometimes I don't have anything to do.
Then I go to sleep or go fishing.

Now the other characters in the first play
will tell you who—or what—they are.

We can't help it.   We are helpless.

Maybe the princess has done something bad. Maybe that is why she is locked in the tower.

There must be some way to get out of this tower . . .

Look! A scissors!

I will call for help. Someone will hear me. Help! Help! HELP!

Someone has heard her all right! Here comes the witch.

Did the princess do something bad? Maybe that is why she is locked in the tower.

You again!

No. The princess is very good.

Oh. How do you know the princess is good?

We know she is good. She has just shared her sandwich with a hungry mouse.

Watch. We will play it for you again.

SNAP

Someone should rescue her.

I don't think a tiny mouse can make this big tower fall down.

Wait and see.

Ha ha

Hee hee hee

Ha ha hee

Tower 2

Tower 3

Tower 1

Nibble, nibble.
Snip snap snee.
The tower falls down.
The princess is free.

That is the end of the play.
You may applaud.

Curtain! Curtain!

We're coming! We're coming!

Coming!

CUR

TAIN

clap   clap   clap   clap   clap

CUR

Everyone come out
and take a bow.

Wait! Wait!

YOU can give the next play at home or anywhere with just three or four friends and you.

All you need is a cat mask to show that
the brother has turned into a cat.
You don't even need that. The brother
says *me-ow*, so you can tell he is a cat.

Maybe you think the cat does not have much to say.
But the person who plays the cat must be a very
good actor. He must show what he is thinking
by the different ways he says *me-ow*.

I am the girl.
If you want the girl
to be a princess,
make a crown for her.

Me-ow. I am really
the girl's brother.
A wizard turned
me into a cat.

I am the
wicked wizard. I cast
magic spells.

I am the mysterious stranger.

I am the girl's grandmother.
I am the brother's
grandmother,
too.

GIRL: Boohoo. Boohoo. Boohoo.

STRANGER: Why are you crying?
            Crying doesn't help.
            I never cry.

GIRL: Boohoo.
            If you never—boohoo—cry—boohoohoo,
            then how do you know if it helps or not?
            Boo hoo hoo!

STRANGER: Stop it, now!
            Stop crying. Maybe I can help you.

GIRL:	Boo hoo hoo hoo.
STRANGER:	It's hard to talk and cry at the same time.
GIRL:	My b-brother—boo hoo hoo hoo!
STRANGER:	*He gives the girl a big handkerchief.* Your brother?
GIRL:	*Points to the Cat.* This is my brother. My little brother.
STRANGER:	Your little brother? He doesn't look a bit like you. He doesn't even look *human*.
GIRL:	Boo hoo boo hoo!
STRANGER:	I didn't mean to hurt your feelings. He's very *nice* looking, really. I've never seen a more handsome . . . uh . . . cat.
GIRL:	He's not a cat. He's my brother.
STRANGER:	Yes. Of course. Your brother.

GIRL:	In a way, he *is* a cat.
	A wizard turned him into a cat.
	And it's all my fault.
STRANGER:	How is it your fault?
GIRL:	I don't know.
	It's just a feeling I have.
	When something bad happens to my brother,
	I feel it's my fault....
	So does he.
CAT:	Meow.
STRANGER:	The wizard must have had some reason
	for turning your brother into a cat.
CAT:	Meow! Meow!
STRANGER:	Begin at the beginning.
	Tell me exactly what happened.
GIRL:	All right.
	This is exactly what happened. Look!

1

Now take this soup home to your poor sick mama. But don't go into the forest. You hear?

Yes, Grandma. I hear you.

2

And if you do go into the forest, you must not eat anything that grows there, or something terrible will happen. You hear me?

Yes, Grandma. Goodbye, Grandma.

3

I have a feeling something terrible is going to happen.

4

I'm hot, too.

I'm hot.

5

I'm hot and I'm tired.

Maybe we can go into the forest for a while. We can rest in the cool shade.

I am the Wicked Wizard.
This is MY forest.
And those are MY berries
your brother is eating.
Now he is in my power!

9

Oh, you darling cat!

But what
will Mama say?
Boohoo.
Boohoo.
Boohoo.

Me-ow.

12

GIRL: So now you know what happened.

STRANGER: Well, I suppose your brother
won't have to be a cat forever.

GIRL: No. Just for 100 years—

CAT: Meee-owWWWWWW!

GIRL: —unless I can break the spell
before the sun goes down today.
But I don't know how to break a spell.

STRANGER: It's lucky for you and your cat—
I mean you and your brother—
that I came along.
I happen to know that
if a spell can be spelled,
it can be unspelled.
That is, the spell can be broken.

CAT: Meow.

STRANGER: All you have to do
to unspell the spell
is to spell it.

GIRL: Spelling is my worst subject.

STRANGER: You will be surprised at what you can do
if you really have to,
or if you really want to.

GIRL: Oh, I want to!

STRANGER: I'll help you.

GIRL: Thank you.

STRANGER: I'll spell the first word for you.
Then you spell it after me.
Saskatchewan: S-A-S-K-A-T-C-H-E-W-A-N.
Now you spell it.

GIRL: S-A-S- hmm. K-A-T- uh ... C-H? *The Stranger nods.*
E-W-A-N!

STRANGER: Good! Very good.
Now try *Kalamazoo* on your own.

GIRL: That's easy: K-A ... L-A ... M-A ....

STRANGER: Yes. What comes next?

GIRL: Oh, help.

STRANGER: *Calls out to the audience.*
Help her, somebody!

SOMEBODY: Z-O-O.

GIRL: Z-O-O.

STRANGER: Only two more words to go!
Kankakee. Spell it quickly.

GIRL: I'm tired.
Spelling gives me a headache.
I have to rest a while.

STRANGER: There's no time to rest.
The sun is going down.
Hurry! We must break the spell
before the sun goes down.

CAT: Meow!

GIRL: Oh dear! *Kankakee:*
K-A-N. hmm ...
K-A-N-K-A?
K-E-E!

STRANGER: Good! Good! Now, *Timbuktu.*
Hurry! Hurry!
The sun is sinking.
I can see only half of it.

GIRL: *Timbuktu.* Oh! I hope I can spell it right.
T-I-M-B-U mmm ... C-H?

 The Stranger frowns.

No! No! Not C-H. K! B-U-K

 The Stranger smiles.

Mmm ... *tu:* T-W-O?

 The Stranger frowns.

T-U!
T-I-M-B-U-K-T-U. *Timbuktu.*

STRANGER: The sun is almost down.
I barely have time
to finish breaking the wizard's spell:
S-C-A-T spells SCAT. *He writes on blackboard.*
Take away the CAT *He crosses it out on blackboard.*
And that leaves *He points.*
your brother!

CAT: ME! *As Cat-Brother pulls off mask and stands up,
he bumps his head against the Stranger's arm.*
OW!

GIRL: Brother!

BROTHER: Sister!

STRANGER: Thank goodness, a happy ending, and just in time! The sun has set.

GIRL: Boo hoo! Boo hoo hoo!

STRANGER: *Now* what?

GIRL: Boohoo! I've always wanted a cat— and now I don't have one anymore. Boohoohoo. **She goes off, pulling her brother by the hand.**

STRANGER: There are days when you can't win! Boo hoo! Boo hoo hoo.

THE END

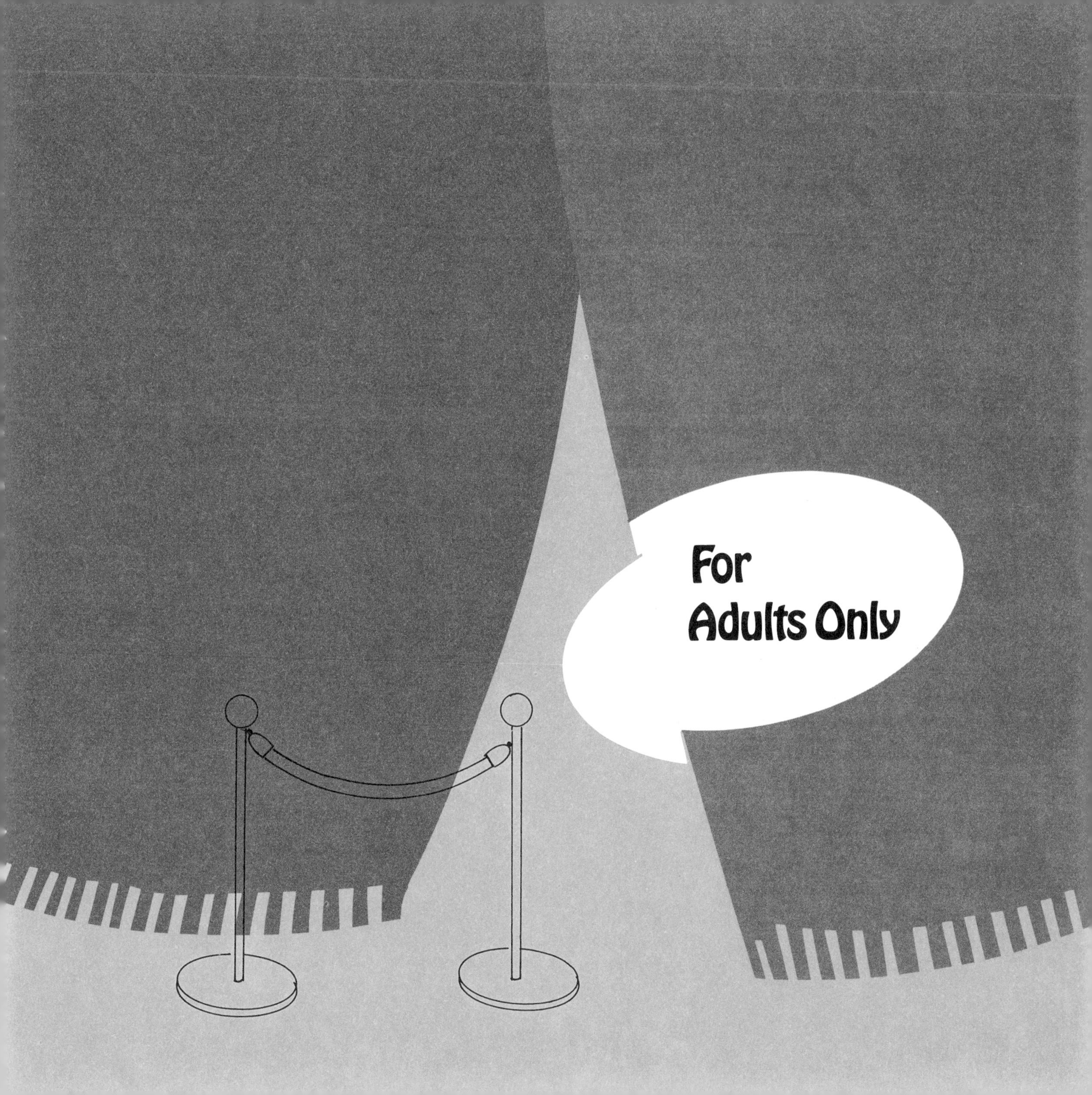
For
Adults Only

Most children are natural actors. What they are likely to lack is a sense of form.

These two plays, with their easy, colloquial text—one of them in comic-book format—are designed to encourage creative dramatization. At the same time they set limits, so that when very young children present one of the plays for friends or for parents, neither the play nor the audience will disintegrate.

The second play, "The Magic Spell" is in more or less conventional script form, but in neither of the plays, once they have read it and entered into the spirit of it, should the children be held to the exact words.

When older children or adult theater groups put on the plays for younger children or for a school assembly or for television, props, music, special effects will suggest themselves.

For example, in "The Magic Spell " a large cardboard sun may be gradually lowered to represent the setting sun, with lights dramatically dimmed as the time limit approaches for un-spelling the magic spell.

Or, in the same play, an experienced acting group may choose to represent the scene in the forest in pantomime on another level (and with three other actors) while the girl describes it to the Mysterious Stranger.

Props and costumes should remain naive in appearance (as indicated in the illustrations), however sophisticated the production.

Last, and most important of all, this book was designed primarily for that limitless stage where all the characters—and the audience, too—are embodied in a single person: the child who reads the book.